Chapter 1

Facing the rushing train, Collin watched as the man walking by him was staring at his phone.

Probably looking at porn, he thought.

Collin smiled at the thought of someone actually being normal for once in their life.

It was just the average day and already Collin found someone that would understand who he was.

It was just a matter of time before there was a guy that caught his eye based on more than his good looking body.

But it seemed that this man was far too busy to even glance in his general direction.

Elizabethan Militia of South Devon (1569AD)

Edited by

Jason D C Sullock

(Devon Family History Society No 4982)

Villages: ASHPRINGTON. PORTLEMOUTH, THURLESTONE, UGBOROUOH, MODBURY, AVETON GIFFORD, HARFORD, KINGSTON, HOLBETON, ERMINGTON, RINGMORE AND BIGBURY

Over 800 names mentioned, most with their weaponry

This booklet, small though it maybe, is dedicated to Flight Lieutenant Charles John Sullock, and all those who defended the Island in another dark hour

The more he thought about it, the more he wondered what the man had to do that kept him so busy.

He was sure that he was going to find the man to be his lover.

He was sure that he was the one that would be in love with the man.

"Excuse me, can anyone tell me the time?"

"7:30. Get a watch."

Chapter 2

That was the first time he had ever spoken to the man that he wanted to fuck like crazy.

He had to have him. He had to get him on a bed, tie him up, put a mask on him, and fuck him until they were both spent.

Then they would be cuddling and he would be happy for all eternity.

But it wasn't easy. Trent was one of those men that took what he wanted and accepted nothing less.

And right now he wanted this man. He shook his head and put his phone away.

As soon as the train pulled up, he took his

single briefcase and climbed aboard.

The sooner they were at the location the better. But the moment he stepped onto the train, he had a feeling something was going to happen.

And it did.

Chapter 3

The more he thought about it, the more he wondered what was going to happen.

Looking down at his ticket, Collin read the numbers and kept an eye on the door that matched his ticket.

When he looked at who was inside, his cock went rock hard.

Shit.

It was Mr. Sexy. This wasn't going to go over well. He knew that this was going to be one tough ass ride.

Literally.

When he opened the door, he heard a rushed sigh before stepping in and putting his own suitcase above his seat and closing the door behind him.

Chapter 4

Trent looked at the man he had been eyeballing before he had moved in front of him, and knew that this was going to be a tough one.

He knew there were curtains on the door. Just as he knew that there would be a lock on the door when the train started moving.

And the fact that he was riding to Saint Louis made things all the more interesting.

It was going to be a long ride, maybe about three to four days.

One thing he knew was this: when they would let everyone enjoy the leisure of the cabin, he was going to strip the man down and fuck him ragged.

Making him moan and scream the name Trent. The thought of it made him rock hard.

God damn it.

Train move faster, he thought.

Chapter 5

The more he thought about it, the more turned on he got.

Damn it, Trent. Hold it together, he thought.

Soon enough the train was moving and the doors were locked.

The bathroom was available to them. But it was two beds, one couch, curtains, and a bathroom between the two of them.

Time to get this going. But it seemed his company beat him to the punch.

"I'm sorry. I forgot to introduce myself," the man said. And that voice of his.

It made Trent's cock throb with need.

He had to have him.

"I'm Collin by the way," he spoke.

And a perfect name to go with such a sexy man. God damn this was going to be fun rush.

Chapter 6

To hell with this, thought Collin, I'm going for it all.

Before he could stop himself, he walked over and leaned towards Trent, meshing their lips together.

The taste was just as amazing as the looks.

Tasted like sugar cookies and cinnamon.

Nothing like that to get a man feel spiced up.

He felt like he could rule the world at this point. But it wasn't going to happen.

He was just going to rule Trent. Everything about him sent the shocking taste of arousal.

And he was going to have him.

Chapter 7

When push came to shove, he was pretty sure he was supposed to be the one dominating this.

And he would.

Trent turned around and shoved Collin against the wall. Trent pressed his chest against Collin's back.

Yanking off Collin's shirt, Trent went to work on kissing that back, from the neck down the back—stopping momentarily to kiss the shoulder blades—and going back up kissing up both sides of Collin.

That brown hair was going to be his. That thin body was going to be fucked senseless.

When he got back down to the top of Collin's jeans, he stopped.

Heading over to his briefcase, he pulled out a mask, and a few ties.

He tossed Collin the mask. "Put it on."

Chapter 8

Making sure the mask was on right; Collin went into the bathroom and looked into the mirror.

He looked like a person that found the finer things in life out of a masquerade ball.

Not that it was a problem for him in the first place.

He had just never done it before. He figured that he was bound to find new things.

When push came to shove, he was pretty damn sure that he was going to let it go.

When he went back into the room, he saw that Trent was standing there, waiting and tapping his foot.

"Don't ever keep me waiting. I don't like waiting. Just pisses me off."

"Sorry," he said.

"And now. I have to punish you."

Chapter 9

Trent liked the sound of his own words. And he would punish him.

Making him get on his hands and knees on the bed—he had pushed the two into one and lowered the curtains—Trent slowly took a moment to admire the view.

He had a man bent over for him. He couldn't believe this was happening. Every possible fantasy was kicking in now.

And his erection wasn't going to wait much longer before it would be exploding.

He went around and tied Collin's hands together with a single tie and tossed the other at his briefcase.

Now it was time to get his fantasy into gear.

Chapter 10

Making sure that he had control of the situation, Collin slid the tie and let Trent tighten it.

He watched as Trent pulled off his jeans and tore off his tight briefs.

"You are going to pay for it."

"I don't give a damn. As long as I can have you that's all that matters."

When he felt the lube slide along his hole, he felt something slide inside him.

A sex toy. A nice dildo. It was a cute blue and seemed to hit all the right spots. Just as he hoped Trent's cock would do.

And he was sure it was going to happen.

Chapter 11

The moans that came out of Collin began to turn him on big time. With every moan, his cock throbbed more and more.

The more he moved the dildo, the more moans came out.

He had to have him. He had to take him now.

Finally pushing Collin on his side and tossing the dildo away, he lay down next to Collin and shoved his cock inside.

"Oh," Collin moaned. "Fuck yeah. Pound my ass with that cock."

"I will if you answer one thing."

"Anything. Just fuck me. Give me that pleasure."

"You have to be mine forever."

"Fine. Whatever you want. Just give it to me."

Chapter 12

Collin kept begging for that cock to fuck him. And fuck him it did. Trent kept pushing in and out eliciting so many moans.

The more Trent thrust, the more Collin moaned. As he kept fucking him, Trent added some extra dirty talking.

"Take it. Yeah."

Every last word gave Collin such ecstasy. He had to keep it going. He had to have him.

Knowing he couldn't take anymore. He rolled off the bed and dragged Trent into the center of the bed.

"Now it's my turn."

"As long as I have you, you will be able to do whatever you want."

"You can have me for the rest of our lives."

Chapter 13

Trent loved it when Collin took over.

He was pulled to the center of the bed and his cock was positioned until it felt the heat of his hole surrounding his cock.

"Oh fuck!" he exclaimed. Nothing could

beat this feeling. Nothing.

But he had a feeling there was going to be more to this.

He pulled the mask off Collin and tossed it aside. As Collin rode him, Trent felt nothing short of euphoria.

The more he rocked back and forth, the more he Trent felt that special ecstasy.

Before he knew it, they were both hollering as they came.

Nothing could make this moment better. Nothing.

Chapter 14

When he climbed off, Collin felt like he had been opened up but frankly he didn't care.

He knew that they would be spending a lot of time together.

And as time began to fly by faster, he was sure they would be happy together.

There came a knock on the door around dinner time.

The two were dressed and everything was fixed up but Collin opened the door.

"Dinner is here," he called over to Trent.

"What's for dinner?"

"Macaroni and cheese with a nice Cole slaw," replied the waiter.

"Sounds good to us. Just put the food on the table."

When he did, Collin slid a twenty into his vest pocket and watched him walk out the door.

"So…what are you going to anyway?" asked Collin before taking a bite of the Cole slaw.

Chapter 15

When they ate, Trent asked Collin all sorts of questions.

"Are you traveling for business or pleasure?"

"Actually Trent—God I love your name—I'm on my way to find a house. I'm moving out of my apartment."

"That's great. I'm heading back home. I just left a business trip and am going back home to do some relaxing. Selling houses is a tough pain in the ass."

"I can understand that. So you are a real estate agent?"

"Actually yes. One of the best. And I do it out of state. What about you? What do you do Collin?”

“I’m a working actor.”

Chapter 16

"That's wonderful," Trent replied.

Collin had never heard a man that seemed to be so excited about being with an actor. Collin had never been that good act acting but he had gone to college for it and now he was trying to find work.

"I want you to call a friend of mine when we get home. He's a director that happens to be looking for new talent to do a movie."

"What do you mean when we get home?"

"I want you to live with me."

"You've got to be kidding me right. We barely know each other. I don't know much about you. How do I know you are not one of those guys that gets all kind of protective over his man? Some kind of a stalker?"

"I guess you don't. But there's only one way to find out."

"How is that?"

Chapter 17

"You have to move in with me and take a chance. You need a place to live; I've been looking for a man to spend my life with. And I choose for it to be you."

"I'm worried. What if we don't work out? What

if I find someone else that I want to be with?"

"There's only one way to find out. Move in with me. And we can make all the love you want."

"I want to fuck and date first."

"That works too," Trent said before they shared their first kiss.

www.ingramcontent.com/pod-product-compliance
Ingram Content Group UK Ltd.
Pitfield, Milton Keynes, MK11 3LW, UK
UKHW020216250726
13967UKWH00001B/23